PARTS of SPEECH

Verb [vurb] Shows action or a state of being. Verbs reveal what is happening in a sentence.

Making.

Noun [nown] Names a person, place, thing, or idea. Nouns are the subject or object of the action in a sentence.

Making friends.

Adjective [aj-ik-tiv] Modifies a noun or pronoun. Adjectives are often placed right in front of the word they modify.

Making new friends.

Adverb [ad-vurb] Modifies a verb, adjective, or other adverb. Adverbs are often made by adding an -*ly* to an adjective.

Bravely making new friends.

Interjection [in-ter-jek-shuhn] A short exclamation. Interjections often express an emotion.

Wow! Bravely making new friends.

WoRD

by

Adam Lehrhaupt

PLAY

illustrated by
Jared Chapman

Arthur A. Levine Books
An Imprint of Scholastic Inc.

Meet Verb.

Verb does things.

She climbs.

She slides.

She twirls.

Everyone watches Verb.
"WOW!" says Interjection.
"An impressive display," says Adjective.
"Very graceful," says Adverb.

Verb is happy.

Meet Noun.

Noun can't DO like Verb.

But Noun can BE.

He can be a person.

Or a place.

Or even a thing.

Now, everyone watches Noun.
"ROAR!" says Interjection.
"Big, scary teeth . . . tiny, little arms,"
says Adjective.
"What will he be next?" says Adverb.

Verb notices.

Noun becomes
this person.

Verb responds.

Noun becomes this place.

Verb reacts.

Noun becomes this thing!

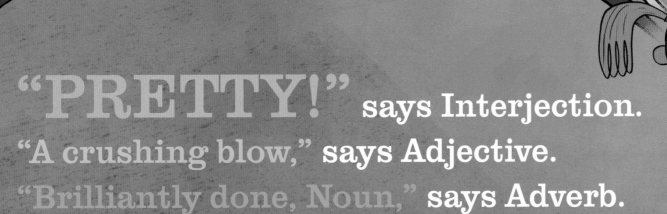

"PRETTY!" says Interjection.
"A crushing blow," says Adjective.
"Brilliantly done, Noun," says Adverb.

Verb sulks. "Why don't you just —"

"BEE!" says Interjection.

"A giant, frightening bee!" says Adjective.
"It's coming dangerously close," says Adverb.

She runs.
Noun doesn't.

"HIDE!"
says Verb.

But Noun can't hide.

Noun can't DO anything.
He is stuck.

The bee flies closer.

Then Verb does something amazing.

She *helps.*

Together, they run.

"**YAY!**" says Interjection.
"So brave!" says Adjective.
"Incredibly heroic," says Adverb.

Then Noun knows just what he'll be to Verb:
a friend.

And Verb knows exactly
what to do with Noun.

King Tut dances.

The unicorn whirls.

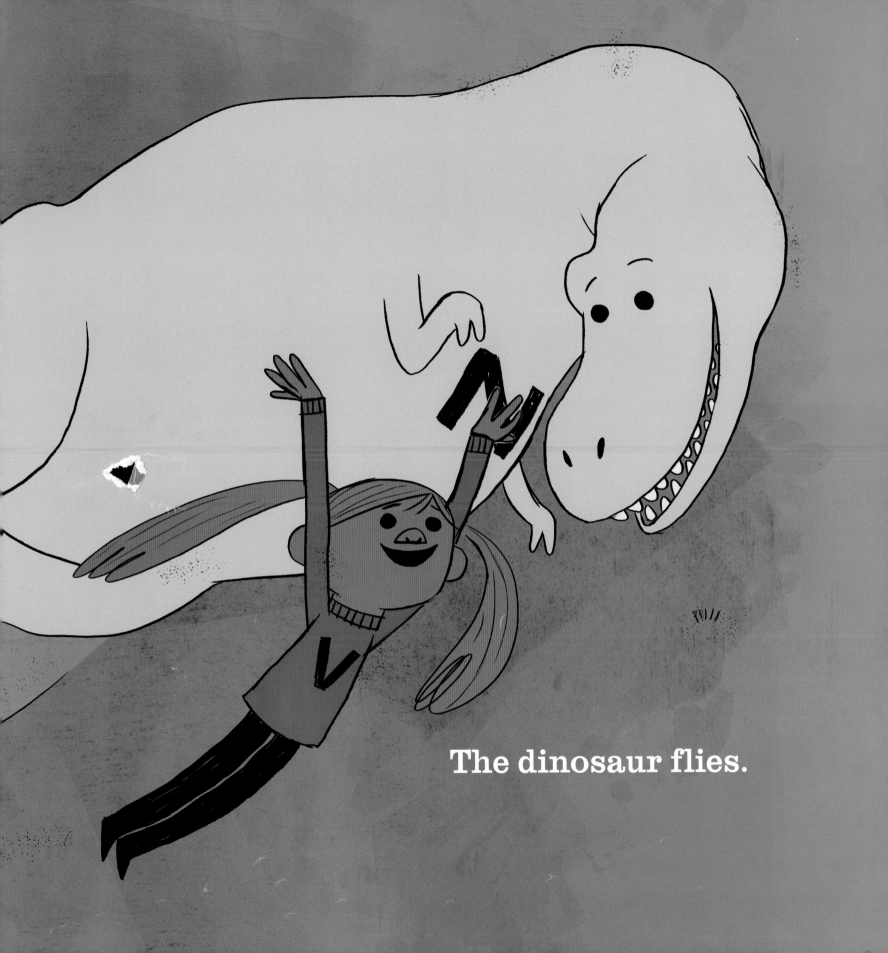

The dinosaur flies.

All the new friends play happily together.
"HOORAY!" says Interjection.

PARTS of SPEECH

Verb [vurb] Shows action or a state of being. Verbs reveal what is happening in a sentence.

Playing.

Noun [nown] Names a person, place, thing, or idea. Nouns are the subject or object of the action in a sentence.

Friends playing.

Adjective [aj-ik-tiv] Modifies a noun or pronoun. Adjectives are often placed right in front of the word they modify.

New friends playing.

Adverb [ad-vurb] Modifies a verb, adjective, or other adverb. Adverbs are often made by adding an -ly to an adjective.

New friends playing happily together.

Interjection [in-ter-jek-shuhn] A short exclamation. Interjections often express an emotion.

Hooray! New friends playing happily together.